SO-AVI-553

Dear Parents and Educators,

Welcome to Penguin Young Readers! As parents and educators, you know that each child develops at his or her own pace—in terms of speech, critical thinking, and, of course, reading. Penguin Young Readers recognizes this fact. As a result, each Penguin Young Readers book is assigned a traditional easy-to-read level (1–4) as well as a Guided Reading Level (A–P). Both of these systems will help you choose the right book for your child. Please refer to the back of each book for specific leveling information. Penguin Young Readers features esteemed authors and illustrators, stories about favorite characters, fascinating nonfiction, and more!

Bones and the Football Mystery

LEVEL **3**

GUIDED READING LEVEL **K**

This book is perfect for a **Transitional Reader** who:
• can read multisyllable and compound words;
• can read words with prefixes and suffixes;
• is able to identify story elements (beginning, middle, end, plot, setting, characters, problem, solution); and
• can understand different points of view.

Here are some **activities** you can do during and after reading this book:
• List all of the words in the story that have an –ed ending. On a separate sheet of paper and using the chart below as an example, write the root word next to the word with the –ed ending.

word with an -ed ending	root word
waved	wave
shouted	shout

• Make Connections: Even though Grandpa's hat is old and dirty and his shirt is too small, he doesn't mind because they're lucky just the way they are. Do you have any items that you keep for good luck?

Remember, sharing the love of reading with a child is the best gift you can give!

—Bonnie Bader, EdM
  Penguin Young Readers program

*Penguin Young Readers are leveled by independent reviewers applying the standards developed by Irene Fountas and Gay Su Pinnell in *Matching Books to Readers: Using Leveled Books in Guided Reading,* Heinemann, 1999.

For Zachary Bienstock,
happy reading. —D.A.A.

To the Newman family football fans.
—B.J.N.

Penguin Young Readers
Published by the Penguin Group
Penguin Group (USA) Inc., 375 Hudson Street, New York, New York 10014, USA
Penguin Group (Canada), 90 Eglinton Avenue East, Suite 700, Toronto, Ontario M4P 2Y3, Canada
(a division of Pearson Penguin Canada Inc.)
Penguin Books Ltd., 80 Strand, London WC2R 0RL, England
Penguin Group Ireland, 25 St. Stephen's Green, Dublin 2, Ireland (a division of Penguin Books Ltd.)
Penguin Group (Australia), 250 Camberwell Road, Camberwell, Victoria 3124, Australia
(a division of Pearson Australia Group Pty. Ltd.)
Penguin Books India Pvt. Ltd., 11 Community Centre, Panchsheel Park, New Delhi—110 017, India
Penguin Group (NZ), 67 Apollo Drive, Rosedale, Auckland 0632, New Zealand
(a division of Pearson New Zealand Ltd.)
Penguin Books (South Africa) (Pty.) Ltd., 24 Sturdee Avenue, Rosebank, Johannesburg 2196, South Africa

Penguin Books Ltd., Registered Offices: 80 Strand, London WC2R 0RL, England

Text copyright © 2012 by David A. Adler. Illustrations copyright © 2012 by Barbara Johansen Newman.
All rights reserved. Published in 2012 by Penguin Young Readers, an imprint of Penguin Group (USA) Inc.,
345 Hudson Street, New York, New York 10014. Manufactured in China.

LIBRARY OF CONGRESS CATALOGING-IN-PUBLICATION DATA
Adler, David A.
Bones and the football mystery / by David A. Adler.
p. cm. — (Bones ; #9)
Summary: When Grandpa's lucky hat goes missing during a college football game, detective Jeffrey
Bones and his friend Sally help look for it.
ISBN 978-0-670-01250-3 (hardcover)
[1. Mystery and detective stories. 2. Hats–Fiction. 3. Lost and found possessions–Fiction. 4. Luck–
Fiction.] I. Title.
PZ7.A2615Bof 2012   [E]—dc23   2011042680

1   3   5   7   9   10   8   6   4   2

BONES
and the Football Mystery

by David A. Adler
illustrated by Barbara Johansen Newman

Penguin Young Readers
An Imprint of Penguin Group (USA) Inc.

Contents

Chapter 1
Grandpa's Lucky Yucky Hat

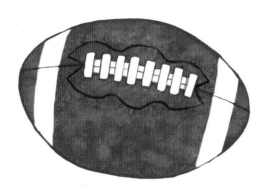

"Your grandpa is cashews
about football," Sally said.

Sally is Grandpa's friend.

"Cashews?" I asked.

"Yes," Sally said.

"Cashews are nuts,
and Grandpa is nuts about football."

Grandpa, Sally, and I were walking
into Donald College Stadium.
"We're going to win today,"
Grandpa told me.
Donald was Grandpa's college.
He always thinks its team
is going to win.

"I brought my lucky shirt,"
Grandpa said when we got to our
seats in the last row.

He took an old shirt from his bag
and put it on.

"That shirt is too small for you,"
Sally said.

"It's lucky," Grandpa told her.

"I wore this shirt the day we won the big game. I was a student then." Grandpa took a hat from his bag. Two ribbons were pinned to it. He put it on.

"Yuck!" Sally said.

"Your hat is old and dirty."

"But it's lucky," Grandpa said.

He took his lucky banner

from his bag and waved it.

"Let's go, Donald!" he shouted.

I brought a bag, too.

It's my detective bag.

A good detective

should always be prepared.

My name is Bones, Jeffrey Bones.

I solve mysteries.

"He's about to kick the ball,"

Grandpa said.

"The game is about to begin."

Chapter 2
Touchdown!

A Donald College player
caught the ball.

"Run! Run!" Grandpa shouted.

The player ran down the field.

Grandpa stood and waved
his banner.

"Pass the ball!" Grandpa called out.

A Donald player threw the ball.

"No! No!" Grandpa shouted.

He sat down and shook his head.

"Did you see that?" he asked us.

"He passed it to the other team!"

Sally took Grandpa's hand.

"Don't get so upset," she said.

"It's only a game."

"But we have to win," Grandpa said.
Sally turned to me and said,
"He's cashews about football."
Suddenly Grandpa stood again
and waved his banner.
A Donald College player ran across
the field holding the ball.

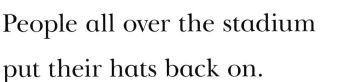

People in the stadium got up
and cheered.

"Touchdown!" Grandpa shouted.

Fans threw their hats into the air.

We all sat down.

"We're winning," Grandpa said.

People all over the stadium
put their hats back on.

"Where's your hat?" Sally asked.

Grandpa looked on the floor.

I looked, too.

The hat wasn't there.

We were sitting in the last row.

I looked behind us.

I saw lots of people buying snacks,
shirts, and programs.

I saw bathrooms and trash cans.

But I didn't see Grandpa's hat.

Chapter 3

Wrappers, Peanut Shells, and Paper Cups

"Probably someone picked up
my hat by mistake," Grandpa said.
"Let's look for someone wearing
a hat with two ribbons."
Sally shook her head.
"No one but you
would wear that hat," she said.

"It's lucky," Grandpa said.

"It's old and dirty," Sally told him.

I opened my detective bag.

I took out my detective glass.

It makes things look bigger.

I looked through the glass.

"Wow!" I told Sally. "You have big eyes."

I looked under our seats.

I found papers and peanut shells.

But I didn't find Grandpa's hat.

Grandpa said,

"Maybe it fell in front."

I walked past Grandpa and Sally

to the row just in front of us.

I told the man at the end of the row,

"I need to get in, please.

I need to find my Grandpa's hat."

The man got up, and I walked past.

I looked under the first seat.

Grandpa's hat wasn't there.

I looked under every seat in the row,

but I didn't find Grandpa's hat.

I went to the next row and the next.

I found lots of wrappers,

peanut shells, and paper cups.

But I didn't find Grandpa's hat.

Chapter 4
I Looked Through My Detective Glass

"I'm sorry," I told Grandpa.

"I didn't find it."

"I know what to do," Sally said.

She left her seat

and walked behind our row.

Maybe Sally is right, I thought.

Maybe the hat fell behind us.

I walked past Grandpa.

I walked among the people

buying snacks, shirts, and programs.

Many of them were wearing hats.

But no one was wearing

Grandpa's lucky hat.

As I walked,

I looked through my detective glass.

I bumped into someone.

Most of his soda spilled on me.

"You should look where
you're going," the man said.

"I am looking," I said.

"I'm a detective, and I'm looking
for my grandpa's hat."

The man threw his empty soda cup in the trash can behind our seats. "Take a look at your grandpa's head," the man told me. "That's where you'll find your grandpa's hat." I looked through my detective glass at Grandpa. The man was right. There *was* a hat on Grandpa's head!

Chapter 5
Clouds and Sky

"I'm glad you found your lucky hat,"
I said when I got back to my seat.
"This hat isn't lucky," Grandpa said.
"The game is almost over,
and we're losing."
I looked at Grandpa
without my detective glass.

"Hey," I said.

"That's not Grandpa's hat."

"Yes it is," Sally told me.

"I bought him a new, clean one."

But where was Grandpa's lucky hat?

I took out my detective pad and pen.

HAT, I wrote on my pad.

UP, I wrote, and looked up.

I saw clouds and sky.

DOWN, I wrote. I looked down.

I saw wrappers, peanut shells, and

paper cups.

Paper cups!

The man who spilled the soda had a paper cup.

Just then I knew what happened to Grandpa's hat.

"I'll be right back,"

I told Grandpa and Sally.

"I'm going to solve a mystery."

Chapter 6
Sometimes Detective Work Is Dirty

Our seats were in the last row.

Right behind us was a trash can.

Grandpa's hat didn't land on the

ground, so it must have landed

in the trash.

I climbed the rail behind our seats.

I looked in the trash.

I saw wrappers, cups,

and half-eaten hot dogs.

I shook the can and saw

something blue. Grandpa's hat!

I reached for it and fell

right into the trash.

The can fell over, and I fell, too.

"Jeffrey!" Grandpa and Sally yelled.

"I found it," I told them.

"I found Grandpa's hat!"

Trash was everywhere.

Grandpa, Sally, and some other
people helped me clean up.

I gave Grandpa his hat.

"Thank you!" Grandpa said.

He gave his new hat to me.

Grandpa put on his old hat.

I looked on the field.

A Donald College player had the ball.

He was running with it.

Players were running after him.

"Go, Donald, go!" people called out.

The player ran all the way
to the end of the field.
"Touchdown!" everyone shouted.
A whistle blew. The game was over.
Donald College had won.
People threw their hats into the air.
Grandpa took off his hat and held it.
"I don't want to lose my lucky hat
again," Grandpa said.

"My new hat is lucky, too," I said.

"I put it on and we won the game."

As we left, Grandpa told Sally,

"When I get home, I'll clean
my lucky hat."

"My new hat is clean," I said.

"But my clothes are not.

Sometimes detective work is dirty!"